波波唸翻天系列 ②

波波的西部冒險記

Justine Korman　著
Lucinda McQueen　繪
本局編輯部　譯

三民書局

For the cast and crew of
"A Bad Day at Gopher's Breath"
—J.K.

獻給 "A Bad Day at Gopher's Breath"
所有幕前幕後的工作人員
—J.K.

For Janine and Kristin, my favorite cowbunnies
Love, Lucy

獻給珍寧和克利斯汀，我最心愛的牛仔兔寶寶
— 愛你們的露西

At the end of the busy Easter season, Sir Byron **gathered** all the Easter bunnies together at the Eggworks Factory. “Once again, it is time to **announce** the **Employee** of the Year,” said the Great Hare. “All of you have worked very hard. But one bunny has gone above and beyond...”

Hopper the grumpy bunny sighed. Speeches were *so* boring.

Then he heard something that made his ears stand straight up.

“And the winner is—Hopper!” said Sir Byron.

“Me?” Hopper **squeaked** happily.

忙碌的復活節季接近了尾聲，拜倫先生聚集所有的復活節兔寶寶到製蛋工廠來。「依照慣例，該是宣布年度最佳員工的時候了，」兔老爹說，「你們大夥兒工作都很賣力。但是有一隻兔寶寶特別特別……」愛抱怨的波波兔嘆了一口氣。這些話有夠無聊。

突然他聽到了讓他耳朵一豎的話。「得獎人是——波波！」拜倫先生說。

「是我？」波波高興地叫了出來。

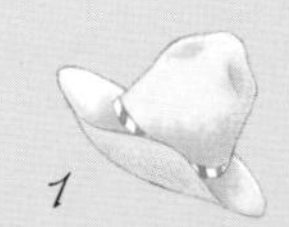

"Yes, you, Hopper," Sir Byron said with a smile. "And this year's prize is a two-week vacation at Slim's **Dude Ranch** out West."

Hopper's ears **drooped**. *A dude ranch!* he thought. *Why would anyone want to go to a* ***dusty*** *old dude ranch?* After long hours painting Easter eggs and **puffing** marshmallow chicks, the only thing Hopper wanted to do was rest and **relax**.

But when he tried to tell Sir Byron he didn't want to go, the Great Hare just said, "No need to thank me, my boy. Enjoy yourself!"

「沒錯，就是你，波波，」拜倫先生微笑著說，「今年的獎品是西部史林觀光牧場雙週假期。」波波的耳朵垂了下來。觀光牧場！他想。怎麼會有人想去塵土漫天的老觀光牧場呢？花了這麼長的時間畫彩蛋和吹小雞雪綿糖，波波現在唯一想做的事就是好好地休息休息、放鬆一下。

但是當他試著告訴拜倫先生他不想去時，兔老爹卻說，「別謝我了，孩子。好好玩吧！」

And in no time at all, Hopper found himself out West and **face-to-face** with one of the biggest bunnies he'd ever seen. The bunny shook Hopper's paw hard enough to hurt, then said in a loud, **jolly** voice, "**Howdy**, stranger! I'm Slim."

一下子，波波便發現自己已經到了西部，並且見到了一個他這輩子見過長得最大個兒的兔子。那隻巨兔用力握痛了波波的手，然後，聽他大聲、愉快地說，「嗨，你好，小客人！我是史林。」

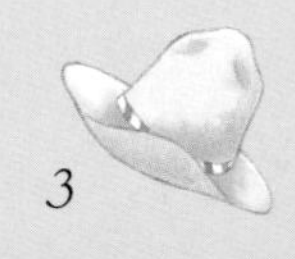

"Let me show you where you'll be bedding down," Slim offered.

After his long, dusty trip, Hopper wanted to sink into a big, soft bed—and not wake up until this silly vacation was over.

"You'll sleep here in the **bunkhouse** for the first week," Slim said. "Then we'll **hit the trail**."

「讓我帶你去看看睡覺的地方，」史林說。

經過漫長、風塵僕僕的旅程後，波波只想癱在一張又大又軟的床上——一直睡到這愚蠢的假期結束為止。

「第一個禮拜，你就睡在這間工作房裡，」史林說。「接下來，我們就要出發啦。」

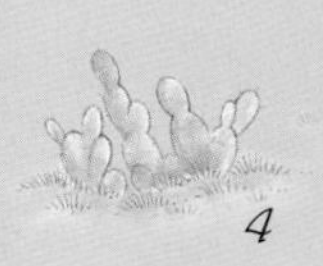

The other **guests** chatted excitedly as they **unpacked**.

Hopper looked around the bunkhouse. No big, soft bed. No TV. The grumpy bunny sighed. *This is going to be a very long two weeks,* he thought sadly.

其他的客人一邊打開行李，一邊興奮地聊天。

波波環顧工作房。沒有大大軟軟的床。沒有電視。這隻愛抱怨的兔子嘆了一口氣。這會是漫長的兩個禮拜，他沮喪地想著。

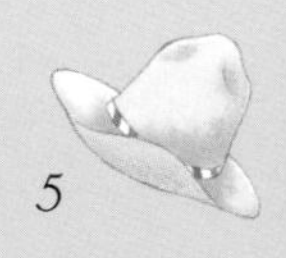

Slim gave each guest a pair of real cowbunny boots, a hat, and a pair of **chaps**. He told them, “While you’re at the ranch, you’ll help out with the **chores**.”

Hopper **frowned**. Who ever heard of doing chores on vacation?

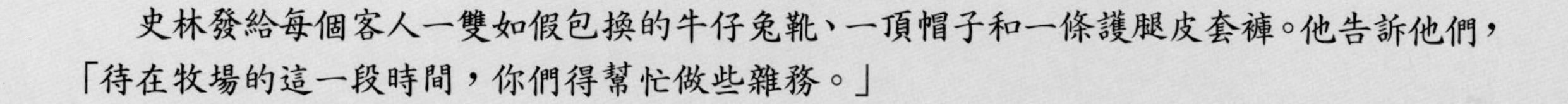

史林發給每個客人一雙如假包換的牛仔兔靴、一頂帽子和一條護腿皮套褲。他告訴他們,「待在牧場的這一段時間,你們得幫忙做些雜務。」

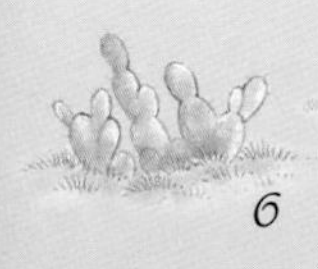

波波眉頭一皺。有誰聽過度假還要打雜的啊？

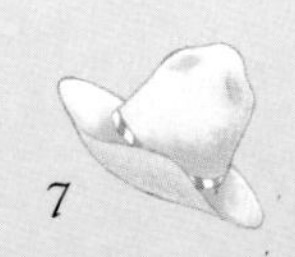

Once they were all in their cowbunny **gear**, Slim gave each guest a horse to ride. “Why don’t you take Ol’ Paint?” Slim said to Hopper. “He’s a nice gentle horse.”

Hopper took the **reins**. Ol’ Paint looked just as bored as the grumpy bunny himself.

他們全都穿戴上了牛仔兔配備後，史林分配給每個客人一匹馬騎。「你騎老潘如何？」史林對波波說。「牠是一匹溫馴的馬哦。」

波波拿起了韁繩。老潘看起來簡直就跟這隻愛抱怨的兔子自己一樣厭倦。

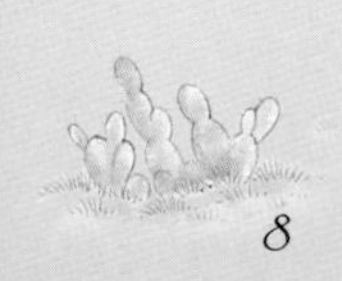

But he **perked** up the minute Hopper climbed into the **saddle**! Everyone laughed when the "gentle" horse threw Hopper all over the **corral**.

Each time the grumpy bunny landed on the ground, Slim said, "Get back up! Remember, a cowbunny never **quits**."

I'm no cowbunny, Hopper thought crankily.

但是當波波一跨上馬鞍，牠的精神就來啦！看到那匹「溫馴」的馬把波波摔得七葷八素，每個人都大笑了起來。

每次這隻愛抱怨的兔子一摔到地上，史林便說，「再上馬！記住，牛仔兔是永不放棄的。」

我又不是牛仔兔寶寶，波波生氣地想。

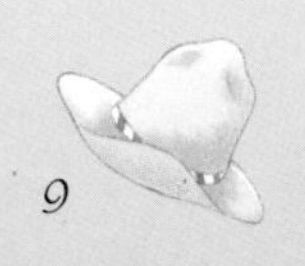

And sure enough, Hopper wasn't any better at shooting with a **bow** and **arrow**, learning to do rope **tricks**, or square dancing.

可以想見的是，波波射箭、學套繩索或跳方塊舞的成果也好不到哪裡去。

*This is the **dumbest** vacation ever,* the grumpy bunny thought grumpily.

這真是有史以來最無聊的假期，這隻愛抱怨的兔子悶悶不樂地想著。

Things got even worse. While everyone else learned how to rope a calf, Hopper only managed to **snag** his own feet.

"I quit!" the grumpy bunny muttered.

But Slim just shook his head. "A cowbunny never quits." He **unwound** the rope from around Hopper's feet. "Be strong! Show that calf who's boss."

Hopper stared at the calf. He **twirled** his rope. He threw it and ...*SWOOSH!* The **lasso** landed around the calf's neck! But before Hopper even had a chance to smile, the calf **yanked** him through the air.

情況愈來愈糟了。當每個人都已經學會用繩子套住小牛時，波波還在設法擺脫纏腳的繩索。「我放棄！」這隻愛抱怨的兔子喃喃地說。但史林只是搖搖頭。「牛仔兔永不放棄。」他解開波波腳上糾結的繩子。「堅強一點！讓那隻小牛知道誰才是老大。」

波波盯著那隻小牛。他揮舞起他的繩索。他一甩……咻！套索套在小牛的脖子上了！但是波波還來不及笑，小牛就猛把他拽上了天。

Slim grinned. "I've never seen a cowbunny get roped before. But don't be **discouraged**. We've got plenty more fun things to do."

Hopper **groaned** as he **staggered** to his feet.

史林咧嘴一笑。「我從來沒看過牛仔兔被套住過。但是別灰心，我們還有很多好玩的事情要做。」

波波一邊埋怨，一邊搖搖晃晃地站了起來。

By the time the day arrived to hit the trail, Hopper was completely **miserable**.

"OK, pardners, saddle up!" called Slim. "Let's keep this **herd** together and move 'em out!"

With a loud "Yee-ha!" the cowbunnies left the ranch.

到了該趕牛上路的那一天，波波更是一副愁眉苦臉的樣子。

「好了，夥伴們，坐穩了！」史林大喊。「讓我們把牛群趕在一起，出發吧！」

在「伊哈！」的吆喝聲中，牛仔兔們離開了牧場。

Hopper soon **discovered** that the only thing he like less than being at the ranch was being on the trail. Every day, the cowbunnies rode from sunup to sunset, moving the large, **mooing** herd.

波波很快就發現他寧可待在牧場，也不想來牧牛。每天，從日出到日落，牛仔兔們都要騎著馬，趕著這一大群哞哞叫的牛。

"This is boring!" Hopper grumbled. "I'm sick of eating beans, tired of listening to stories, and I never, ever want to sing another song around a **campfire**!"

「真是無聊！」波波抱怨著。「我已經厭倦了吃豆子、聽故事，而且我再也不想圍在營火旁唱歌了！」

One morning, Slim said, “I’ve got a special treat for you cowbunnies! Today we’re going to visit an old gold **mine**.”

“Yee-ha!” the other guests cried happily.

有一天早上，史林說，「我為你們這些牛仔兔準備了一個特別節目！今天我們要去參觀一座舊的金礦坑。」

「伊哈！」其他的客人都開心地歡呼起來。

But not Hopper. His tail was **sore** from riding.

He was *really* sick of beans. And, most important, the mine looked **scary**. "It's too dark to see anything in there," the trembling bunny **objected**.

Slim **chuckled** and handed Hopper a flashlight.

"Come along, pardner," he said. "A cowbunny never walks away from something just because he's scared."

波波可沒那麼開心。他的尾巴騎馬騎到痛了。他吃膩了豆子。而且，最重要的是，那座礦坑看起來怪嚇人的。「那裡面太暗了，什麼都看不到，」發抖的波波抗議著。

史林笑著，交給波波一支手電筒。

「來吧，夥伴，」他說。「牛仔兔絕不會因害怕而逃避的。」

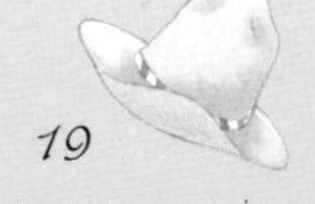

Hopper stepped into the dark mine.

"I want y'all to **grab** a pardner's paw," Slim told the group. "This here mine has more **twists and turns** than a **porcupine** has **quills**. Some even say it's **haunted** by the ghosts of miners who took a wrong turn and never found their way out."

波波踏進了黑暗的礦坑。

「我要你們大家手牽手，」史林告訴大家。「這座礦坑的坑道彎道數目比豪豬的刺還多。甚至還有人說這裡鬧鬼，那些鬼魂是轉錯彎，再也走不出去的礦工的魂魄。」

Hopper **shuddered**. Suddenly, something **screeched** right by his ear. *"Eeeeek!"* Hopper screamed and started to run out of the mine.

"Wait! It was only a bat. He won't hurt you," Slim called after him. But the grumpy bunny had seen enough of the ghostly gold mine.

"I'll wait outside," Hopper said in a shaky voice.

波波嚇得直發抖。突然，有個東西就在他耳邊發出吱吱聲。「唉呀！」波波尖叫了起來，開始轉身往坑外跑。

「等一下！只不過是隻蝙蝠罷了。牠不會傷害你的，」史林在他背後喊著。但是這隻愛抱怨的兔子已經看夠這個陰森森的金礦坑了。

「我在外面等，」波波顫抖地說。

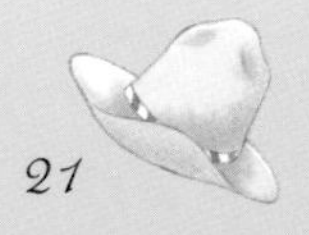

Before the cowbunnies hit the trail again, Slim counted the cattle. "We're one calf short!" he exclaimed.

"Ringo's missing," one of his helpers realized.

"We've got to find that calf," Slim said. "Everybody spread out and start looking!"

在牛仔兔們再度趕牛上路之前，史林數了數牛隻。「我們少了一頭小牛！」他大喊。

「鈴哥不見了，」他的一名助手弄清楚後說。

「我們得去找這隻小牛，」史林說。「大家分頭開始去找吧！」

Hopper wandered around, **halfheartedly** looking for Ringo. Soon he found himself outside the mine.

The grumpy bunny peered inside just in time to catch a **glimpse** of a cow's tail **disappearing** into the blackness.

Hopper's stomach dropped like a **bucket** down a deep well. He wanted to go for help, but he knew Ringo might be hopelessly lost by the time he returned.

The grumpy bunny thought hard. No one would know if he just **pretended** not to have seen the calf at all. But, scared as he was, Hopper couldn't leave poor Ringo all alone in that **spooky** mine.

波波晃來晃去，漫不經心地尋找鈴哥。很快地他發現自己來到了礦坑外。這隻愛抱怨的兔子往裡面一看，正巧瞥見一條牛尾巴消失在黑暗中。波波的胃直往下沈，就像水桶掉進深井裡一樣。他想去找人幫忙，但是他知道等到他回來的時候，鈴哥可能完全不知去向了。這隻愛抱怨的小兔子想了又想。如果他裝作根本沒看到小牛的話，也不會有人知道。但是，儘管他害怕，波波還是不能讓可憐的鈴哥孤獨地留在那陰森森的礦坑中。

Hopper took a deep breath and **marched** into the mine. *Eeek! Eeek! Shriek!* Bats **squeaked** all around Hopper's ears. He ran back to the entrance. But Slim's words wouldn't stop **echoing** in Hopper's mind: *A cowbunny never walks away from something just because he's scared.*

波波深深地吸了一口氣，便大步走進了礦坑裡。

吱！吱！咯吱！蝙蝠們在波波的耳邊尖聲叫著。他跑回入口處。但是史林的話不停地在波波心裡回響著：牛仔兔不會因害怕而逃避。

Hopper headed back into the darkness. He followed a low moo down a narrow **passage**, and there, right in front of him, was Ringo!

Hopper swung his rope. *Swoosh!* It fell over Ringo's head and **slipped** down around his neck.

"I did it!" Hopper shouted—just as Ringo **bolted**.

波波回頭走進黑暗裡。他跟著低低的哞哞聲，沿著一條狹窄的通道走，鈴哥就在那裡，就在他的正前方！

波波甩著手中的繩子，咻的一聲！繩子掉在鈴哥的頭上，滑落到牠的脖子上。

「我成功了！」波波大叫——這時鈴哥卻狂奔了起來。

"Oh, no, you don't!" Hopper held the rope with all his might. "I'm the boss here," he told the calf firmly.

After that, Ringo was happy to follow Hopper back to camp. The calf was even happier to see his **relieved** mother.

Slim **beamed** with pride. "I **reckon** you're a true cowbunny after all, Hopper."

「喔，不，你別這樣！」波波用盡全力抓住繩子。「這裡我最大，」他堅決地告訴那頭小牛。

之後，鈴哥就高高興興地跟波波回營地。小牛見到鬆了一口氣的牛媽媽就更開心了。
史林驕傲地微笑著。「我認為你真不愧是個貨真價實的牛仔兔呢，波波。」

Hopper could hardly believe his ears. For the rest of the day, he didn't even think about his sore tail. Instead, he made up a song about being a real cowbunny:

A cowbunny may fall off his horse
and land in a gopher pit;
He might get snared in his own lasso
or be scared out of his wits.
But as long as there's sand in sandwiches,
a cowbunny must have ***grit****.*
For a cowbunny can do anything,
'cause a cowbunny never quits!

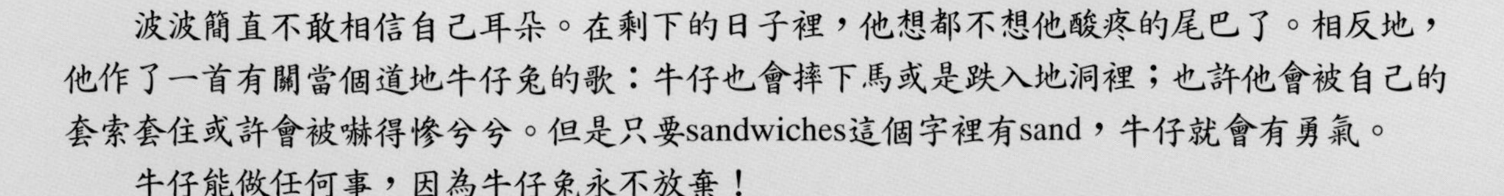

波波簡直不敢相信自己耳朵。在剩下的日子裡，他想都不想他酸疼的尾巴了。相反地，他作了一首有關當個道地牛仔兔的歌：牛仔也會摔下馬或是跌入地洞裡；也許他會被自己的套索套住或許會被嚇得慘兮兮。但是只要sandwiches這個字裡有sand，牛仔就會有勇氣。

牛仔能做任何事，因為牛仔兔永不放棄！

When Hopper finished singing,
all the cowbunnies **cheered**.

當波波唱完後，所有的牛仔兔都歡呼了起來。

Later, Hopper **snuggled** into his bedroll. The grumpy bunny no longer minded sleeping under the stars **twinkling** in the big western sky. In fact, Hopper looked for the brightest one and whispered, “I wish this vacation would never end!”

稍晚，波波鑽進睡袋裡，這隻愛抱怨的兔子不再介意睡在星光閃爍的大西部星空下了。事實上，波波找到了最亮的一顆星，並低聲地說，「我希望這次假期永遠不要結束！」

A

announce [ə`naʊns] 動 宣布

arrow [`æro] 名 箭

B

beam [bim] 動 笑顏逐開

bolt [bolt] 動 狂奔出去

bow [bo] 名 弓

bucket [`bʌkɪt] 名 水桶

bunkhouse [`bʌŋk,haʊs] 名 工寮

C

campfire [`kæmp,faɪr] 名 營火

chaps [tʃæps] 名 護腿皮套褲

cheer [tʃɪr] 動 喝采

chore [tʃor] 名 日常雜務

chuckle [`tʃʌkl̩] 動 竊笑

corral [kə`ræl] 名 畜欄

D

disappear [,dɪsə`pɪr] 動 消失

discourage [dɪs`kɝɪdʒ] 動 使氣餒

discover [dɪ`skʌvɚ] 動 發現

droop [drup] 動 下垂

dude [dud] 名 （到西部旅遊的）東部都市人

dumb [dʌm] 形 無趣的

dusty [`dʌstɪ] 形 滿是灰塵的

E

echo [`ɛko] 動 回響

employee [,ɛmplɔɪ`i] 名 員工

F

face-to-face [`fes tə `fes] 形 面對面的

frown [fraʊn] 動 皺眉頭

gather [`gæðɚ] 動 聚集

gear [gɪr] 名 用具，裝備

glimpse [glɪmps] 名 一瞥

grab [græb] 動 抓住

grit [grɪt] 名 勇氣

groan [gron] 動 埋怨

guest [gɛst] 名 旅客

halfheartedly [`hæf`hartɪdlɪ] 動 不熱心地

haunt [hɑnt] 動 （鬼魂等）出沒

herd [hɝd] 名 牛群

hit the trail 出發

howdy [`haʊdɪ] 名 嗨！你好！

jolly [`dʒɑlɪ] 形 愉快的

lasso [`læso] 名 套索

march [mɑrtʃ] 動 前進

mine [maɪn] 名 礦坑

miserable [`mɪzrəbḷ] 形 悲慘的

moo [mu] 動 哞哞地叫

object [əb`dʒɛkt] 動 反對

passage [`pæsɪdʒ] 名 通道

perk [pɝk] 動 恢復精神 《up》

porcupine [`pɔrkjə,paɪn] 名 豪豬

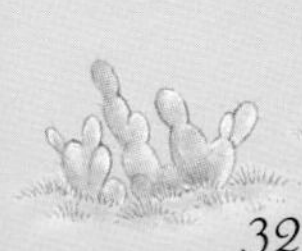

pretend [prɪ`tɛnd] 動 假裝

puff [pʌf] 動 使鼓起

quill [kwɪl] 名 硬毛，刺

quit [kwɪt] 動 停止

ranch [ræntʃ] 名 牧場

reckon [`rɛkən] 動 認為

rein [ren] 名 繮繩

relax [rɪ`læks] 動 休息

relieved [rɪ`livd] 形 寬心的

saddle [`sædl̩] 名 馬鞍

scary [`skɛrɪ] 形 可怕的

screech [skritʃ] 動 發出尖銳的聲音

shudder [`ʃʌdɚ] 動 發抖

slip [slɪp] 動 滑落 《down》

snag [snæg] 動 鉤住

snuggle [`snʌgl̩] 動 舒服地躺著

sore [sɔr] 形 酸痛的

spooky [`spukɪ] 形 陰森森的

squeak [skwik] 動 吱吱地尖叫

stagger [`stægɚ] 動 蹣跚

trick [trɪk] 名 絕技

twinkle [`twɪŋkl̩] 動 閃爍

twirl [twɝl] 動 揮動

twists and turns 彎曲

unpack [ʌn`pæk] 動 解開，打開

unwind [ʌn`waɪnd] 動 解開，鬆開

yank [jæŋk] 動 用力拉

個兒不高・志氣不小・智勇雙全・人人叫好

我是大喜，別看我個兒小小，

我可是把兇惡的噴火龍耍得團團轉！
連最狡猾的巫婆也大呼受不了呢！
想知道我這些有趣的冒險故事嗎？

中英對照

大喜說故事系列

Anna Fienberg & Barbara Fienberg／著
Kim Gamble／繪　王秋瑩／譯

每本均附CD
（本系列陸續出版中）

國家圖書館出版品預行編目資料

波波的西部冒險記 / Justine Korman著;Lucinda McQueen繪;[三民書局]編輯部譯.－－初版一刷.－－臺北市;三民,民90
面;公分--(探索英文叢書.波波唸翻天系列;2)
中英對照
ISBN 957-14-3441-8 (平裝)
1.英國語言—讀本

805.18 90003945

網路書店位址 http://www.sanmin.com.tw

著作人 Justine Korman
繪　圖 Lucinda McQueen
譯　者 三民書局編輯部
發行人 劉振強
著作財產權人 三民書局股份有限公司
臺北市復興北路三八六號
發行所 三民書局股份有限公司
地址／臺北市復興北路三八六號
電話／二五〇〇六六〇〇
郵撥／〇〇〇九九九八——五號
印刷所 三民書局股份有限公司
門市部 復北店／臺北市復興北路三八六號
重南店／臺北市重慶南路一段六十一號
初版一刷 中華民國九十年四月
編　號 S 85590
定　價 新臺幣壹佰捌拾元
行政院新聞局登記證局版臺業字第〇二〇〇號

ISBN 957-14-3441-8 (平裝)